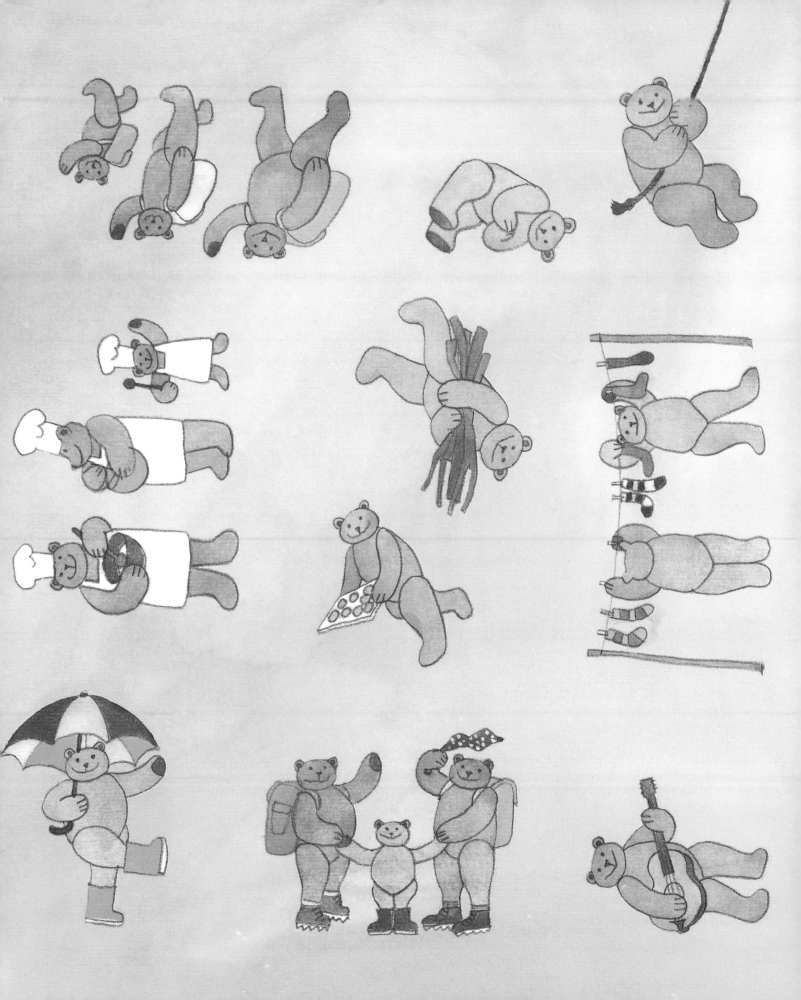

First Paperback Edition 1996

Copyright © 1994 by Martina Selway

Published by Ideals Children's Books
An imprint of Hambleton-Hill Publishing, Inc.
Nashville, Tennessee 37218

First published in the United Kingdom in 1994 by
Hutchinson Children's Books
Random House UK Limited
20 Vauxhall Bridge Road, London SW1V 2SA

Printed in China

Library of Congress Cataloging-in-Publication Data

Selway, Martina
        Wish you were here / Martina Selway.
            p.   cm.
        Summary: Through letters to her relatives at home, Rosie
reveals that her negative feelings about camp gradually change
as the weather improves and she makes friends.
        ISBN 1-57102-032-2 (trade)—ISBN 1-57102-040-3 (paper)
        [1. Camps—Fiction. 2. Letters—Fiction.] I. Title.
PZ7.S464Wi   1996
[E]—dc20   94-31995
                                                                CIP
                                                                AC

Wish
You Were Here

Martina Selway

Ideals Children's Books • Nashville, Tennessee

For Edna and Ted Price

Rosie is going away to camp.
Mom says she'll love it.
Grandad says she'll love it.
Aunty Mabel says she'll love it.
Rosie would rather stay home.

Dear Mom,
    The bus ride was very bumpy and I felt sick.
The driver stopped the bus, but when I got out
I felt better, so we started off again. Then
Sarah felt sick.
Miss West said, "Let's all sing a song."
Sarah's face went funny and white. Then
she _was_ sick! It went all over my new
sneakers.
I don't want to go to camp.

Love from
        Rosie

Dear Grandad,
   When we got to the camp, it was raining and there was mud everywhere. Danny Fisher pushed Roland and he slipped into a huge puddle.

He was covered in mud.

Mr. Granville said, "Rule number one: don't get wet! It's difficult to dry things out when it's raining."
I think Roland was crying.
I don't like Mr. Granville.
Love from Rosie

Dear Aunty Mabel,
  We are staying in this big smelly old cabin because it's too wet to sleep in the tents. I'm sharing bunks with Sarah, but I don't mind because she's brought lots of crackers with her. Danny kept trying to scare us. Miss Jones said, "Stop making those silly noises, Danny. You're not frightening anyone."
But we were frightened.
I don't like it in here.

Love Rosie

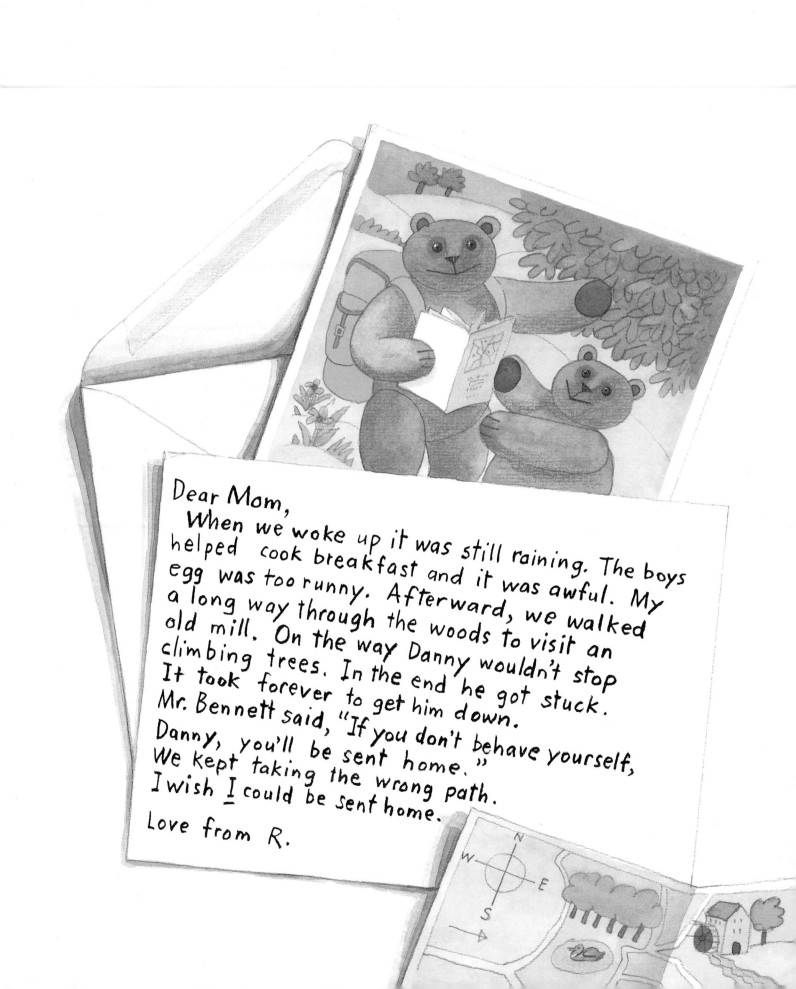

Dear Mom,
   When we woke up it was still raining. The boys helped cook breakfast and it was awful. My egg was too runny. Afterward, we walked a long way through the woods to visit an old mill. On the way Danny wouldn't stop climbing trees. In the end he got stuck. It took forever to get him down. Mr. Bennett said, "If you don't behave yourself, Danny, you'll be sent home." We kept taking the wrong path. I wish I could be sent home.

Love from R.

Dear Grandad,
    The old mill was great! We watched grain being ground up to make flour. Everyone there was dressed up in old-fashioned clothes and looked very funny. Afterward, they gave us a tray of raisin biscuits made from the flour. Danny Fisher took two and licked them both. Miss West said, "Not two, Danny. Give one of those to Rosie."
    I didn't want one.
    I didn't want a biscuit that <u>he'd</u> licked.
                Love from Rosie

Dear Aunty Mabel,
   The teachers made a rope swing across the stream today and everyone took a turn, except Sarah.
I tried and tried, but I couldn't get over.
I kept landing in the water.
Roland Roberts said, "Rule number one: don't get wet!"
Everybody laughed, but I didn't think it was very funny.
I think I've got a cold.

   Love R.

Dear Grandad,
 It's stopped raining at last and we're going to sleep in the tents tonight. Yippee! Now Sarah says she doesn't want to because there might be creepy crawlies. Miss West told her that nothing could possibly harm her.
Danny Fisher said, "Only slugs and snails and spiders and snakes!"
Sarah started to cry and Danny had to go see Mr. Granville.
I hope there aren't any creepy crawlies.

        Love from Rosie.

Dear Mom,
  We've just been to a blacksmith's shop to watch him shoe a horse. When the shoe went on the horse's hoof, it was still hot. It didn't hurt him, but you could smell the hoof burning. It was horrible.
  Mr. Bennett said, "It smells like Mr. Granville's socks."
  Guess what? When we got outside the sun was shining.
  I think we're having cheeseburgers for lunch.

  Love from Rosie.

Dear Grandad,
   We woke up so early this morning. It was still dark. We lay in our beds talking until it got light and the birds started singing. Miss Jones said, "Okay girls, who's going to help me make breakfast?" We all yelled ME. We made French toast. It was wonderful!
I'm getting used to camp now.
      Love from Rosie.

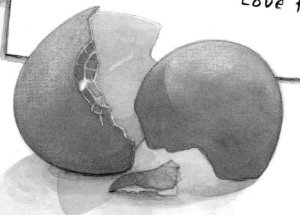

Dear Aunty Mabel,
  After dinner today we built a big campfire. Mr. Granville played his guitar and we all sat around and sang songs. We stayed up really late until all the wood had burned away.

Miss West said, "Come on sleepyheads, off to bed for you."

She let us go to bed without washing our faces.

I really like this camp.

Love from R.

Dear Mom,

I did it! I crossed the stream on the rope and Mr. Granville gave me a star. After lunch we're going to make a raft from logs. Tomorrow we're going to visit some caves. I can't wait. Danny Fisher said, "Come on, Tarzan. It's my turn next."

I'm having the best time ever. Wish you were here.

Lots of love from

Rosie. X

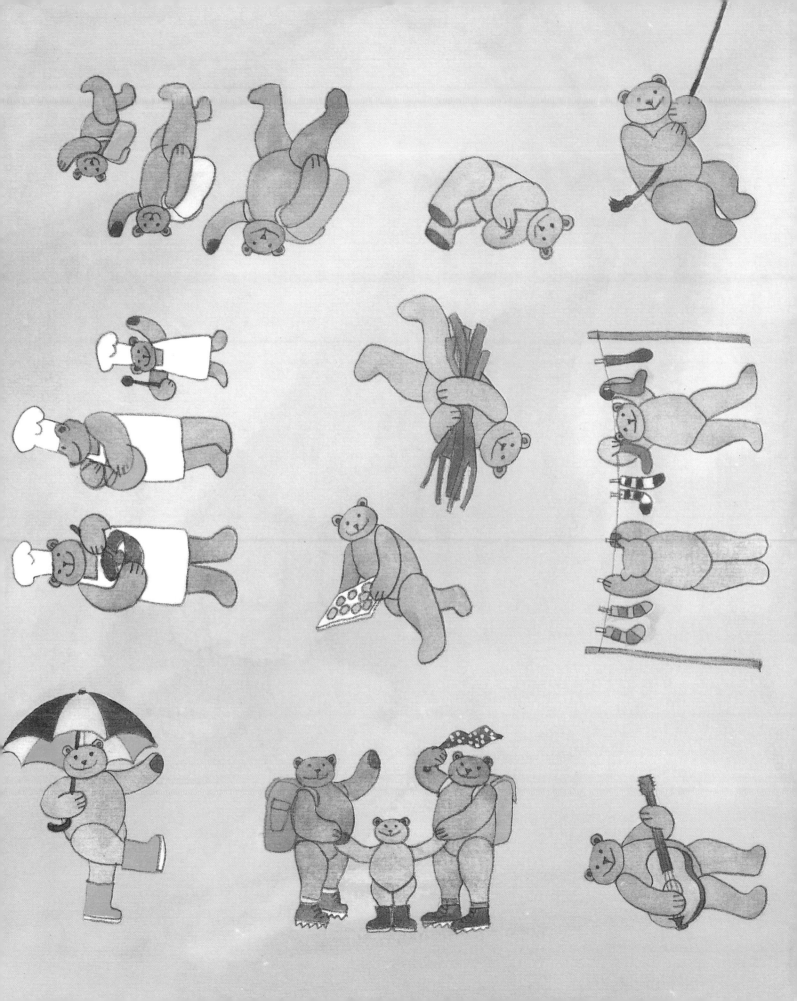